A Lullaby For Daddy

A Lullaby For Daddy

Written by Edward Biko Smith
Illustrated by Susan Anderson

Africa World Press, Inc.

P.O. Box 1892
Trenton, New Jersey 08607

Africa World Press Inc.
P.O. Box 1892
Trenton NJ 08607

Copyright © 1994, Edward Biko Smith

Cover and Book Illustrations
Copyright © 1994, Susan Anderson

Book Production coordinated at Africa World Press, Inc. by Carles J. Juzang

First Printing, 1994

Library of Congress Cataloging - in - Publication Data

Smith, Edward Biko.
    A lullaby for Daddy / written by Edward Biko Smith ; illustrated
by Susan Anderson.
        p. cm
    Summary: A little girl and her father compose a lullaby at
bedtime.
    ISBN 0-86543-403-4 (cloth) :. -- ISBN 0-86543-404-2 (paper).
    [1. Bedtime--Fiction. 2. Lullabies--Fiction. 3. Fathers and
daughters--Fiction. 4. Afro-Americans--Fiction.] I. Anderson,
Susan, ill. II. Title.
PZ7.S6449Lu 1994
[E] --dc20   94-9773
                                                       CIP
                                                        AC

Printed in Hong Kong by Annboli and Bornmore Limited

For Aliya

Rosie loved to play with her little keyboard. It was special to her because it was like the one Daddy used at work. Tonight, Rosie heard singing. It sounded like Daddy.

Rosie crept to the banister and looked
over the top. Daddy was singing to Mommy.
Rosie could see that Mommy was very happy.

When Rosie went downstairs to play, Daddy said, "Honey, it's late, let's get ready for bed." So Rosie put away her books and kissed Mommy goodnight.

Daddy was very big.
He picked Rosie up,
folded her into his arms
and carried her upstairs.

While Rosie brushed her teeth Daddy filled the tub.
"It's time to take your bath Rosie," he said.

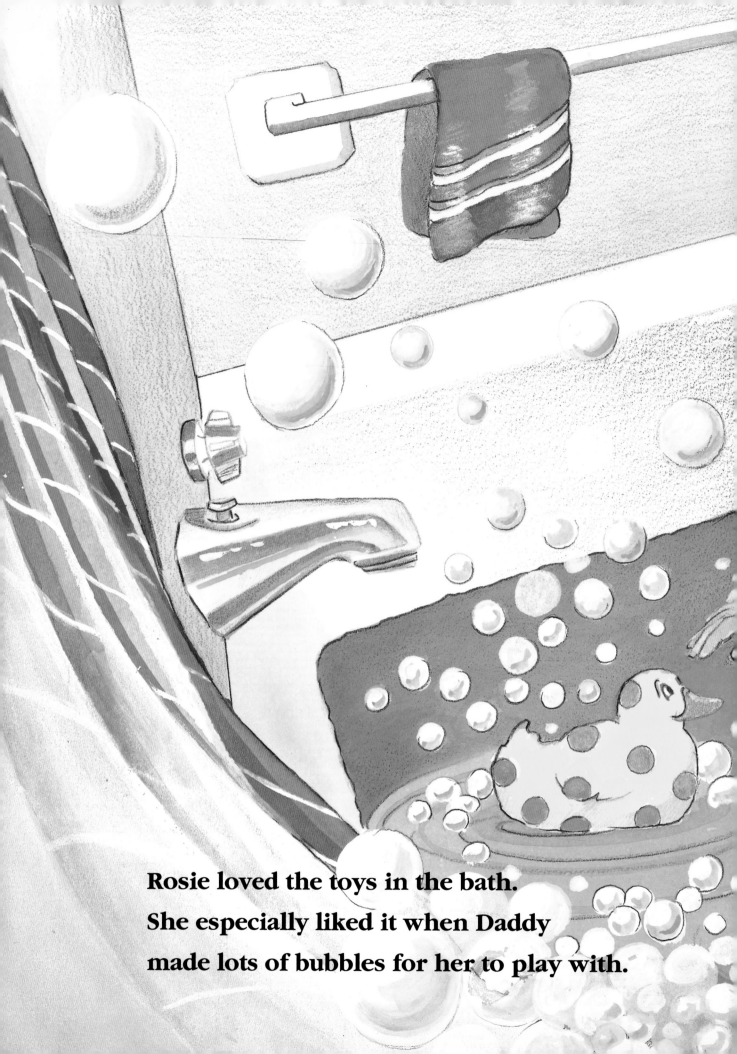

Rosie loved the toys in the bath.
She especially liked it when Daddy
made lots of bubbles for her to play with.

Rosie dried off in a big towel
and snuggled on Daddy's lap.

She thought Daddy was wonderful and when she remembered him singing to Mommy, it gave her an idea.

"I want to make a song for you Daddy. Will you help me ?," Rosie asked. She touched the keys and liked the sounds they made. Daddy sang some words: "soft as a kiss…night falls…good night baby…sleep tight baby."

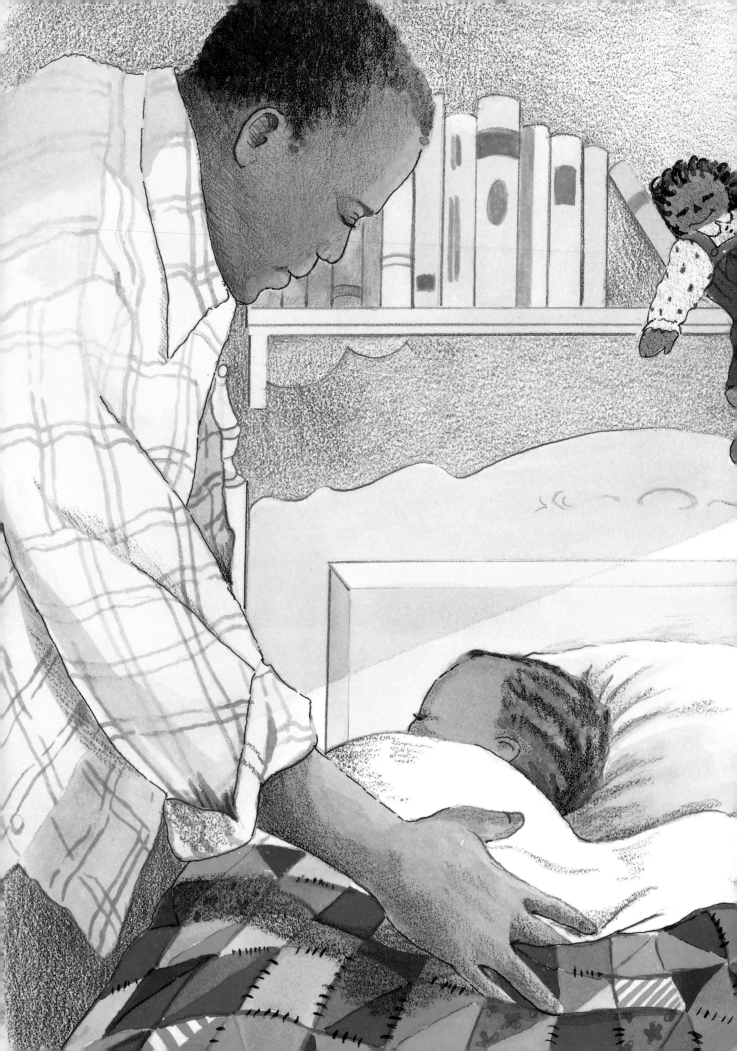

The song made Rosie sleepy
so Daddy tucked her into bed.

The next day while Mommy and Daddy were at work, Rosie went to stay at Mrs. Bryan's house. She had lots of fun playing with her friends.

That night Rosie helped Mommy clean up after dinner. She told Mommy about the song she had made with Daddy. Mommy said it sounded like a lullaby.

When bedtime came again Rosie had a
surprise for Daddy. She remembered
the words to their song.

They sang it together
on the way upstairs.

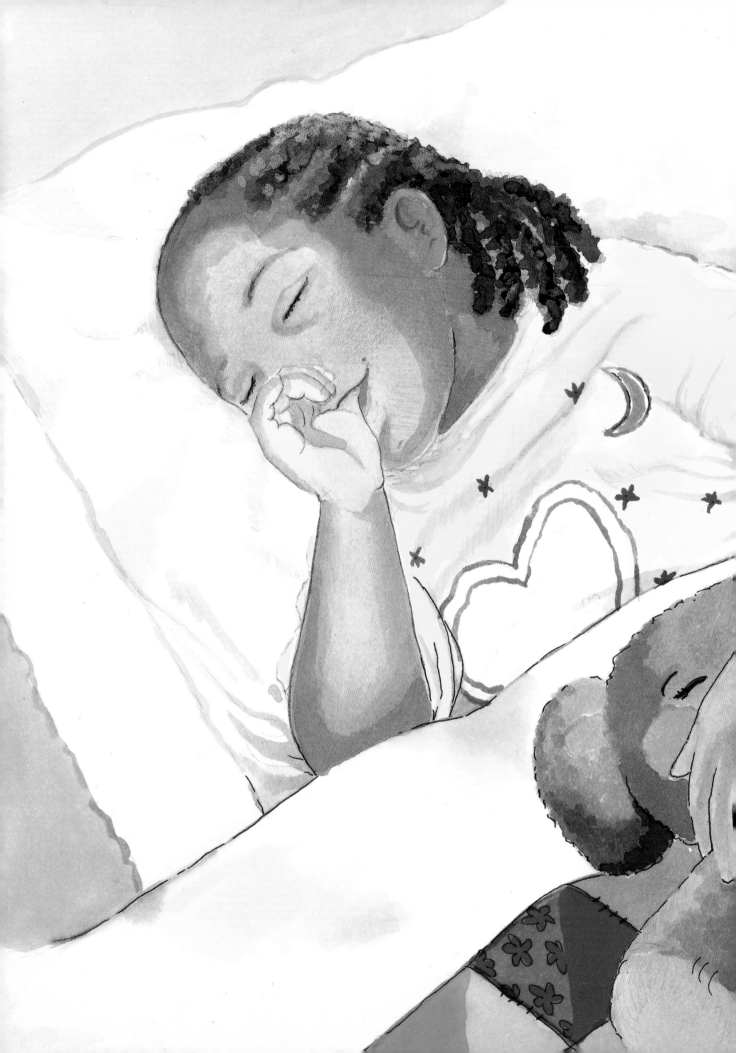

Rosie drifted into sleep as Daddy's gentle voice sang the lullaby that they had made. Rosie felt very happy.

Rock - a -bye